# THE ADVENTURE OF FOOT, FOOTFOOT, AND FOOTFOOTFOOT

P.B. Greenway

Printed in the United States of America

ISBN 979-8-89114-074-5 (hc)
ISBN 979-8-89114-073-8 (sc)
ISBN 979-8-89114-075-2 (e)

Library of Congress Control Number: 2024904767

2024.05.21

MainSpring Books
5901 W. Century Blvd
Suite 750
Los Angeles, CA, US, 90045

www.mainspringbooks.com

# Chapter one

# "Getting past Mother"

Foot got up real early so he could make sure they had all of the things he thought they might need before Mother Rabbit got up. Foot was the oldest of the three. That being the case he always took the leader role in what ever they were getting into which was usually trouble. So he had to move fast so mother wouldn't catch him. So he figured not waking Footfoot and Footfootfoot would be the best way not to. Foot was not the smartest of the three; he just tried to think about everything and was cautious. The smartest of the three would have to be Footfoot, he can figure out anything. Which was how to keep them from getting caught or out of some kind of trouble they managed to get in some how. He was three minutes younger than Foot and two minutes older than Footfootfoot. Now Footfootfoot was the carefree one of the brothers, he wasn't scared to do anything. That usually adds to the stress of Foot's role as leader always having to keep an eye on him. Foot got everything they needed and hide it at the edge of the field, just in the nick of time to. When he got back in the house mother was just getting up so he hurried to their room and acted like he was just then getting up too.

"Good morning mother", said Foot. "Yes it is and what would you like for breakfast", ask Mother Rabbit.

"I'm not sure let me wake up Footfoot and Footfootfoot and see what they would like", said Foot

"Ok, mother said, but hurry up so I can get done with it I've got a long day planned working in the garden. I might even need some help." Oh my goodness thought Foot I've got to get Footfoot up he's going to have to come up with a getting out of helping plan.

So Foot ran to wake them. He told them what mother had said about working in the garden and might need our help.

"Even if she doesn't need out help we've got to get started before she get to the garden or she will see all the stuff I hide, you can see it from the garden", said Foot.

"Think of something while I tell mother what we want for breakfast Footfoot". Said Foot.

"Make it a big breakfast so I will have more time to think of something", replied Footfoot.

Once again Footfoot had done it. He decided we could tell mother we had already promised Mr. Groundhog we would

help him in his garden and he was going to take us fishing
for helping him. And it workout great, she even packed us
a picnic for when we went fishing. So right after breakfast
they ran outside and gathered up their stuff and headed out
before mother got to the garden.

# Chapter two

## "The big field"

The field seemed to go on forever, Footfootfoot ran on ahead as usual leaving Foot and Footfoot carrying everything.

"Lets stop and rest a minute", said Footfoot.

"We will when we catch up to Footfootfoot, there is no telling what he's into by now", replied Foot.

When they got to Footfootfoot he was staring at a hole in the ground. "What did you find", ask Foot?

"There is something in this hold, ya'll come and look", replied Footfootfoot.

'How do you know there is something in it, did you see it go in", ask Footfoot?

"No, but I saw something moving in it when I found it and I've been watching for it again", replied Footfootfoot.

"Get a stick and poke down in it", said Footfoot.

"No you don't know what in there it can be a snake for all you know", said Foot.

"Ah your just chicken, hey Footfoot hand me that stick beside you", said Footfootfoot.

And Foot was right to, they had no idea what was in that hold and by the time they found out it was to late. Bees were every where and when they finally stop running and dodge bees trying not to get sung they had lost all of their supplies and a mile away.

# Chapter three

# "The Woods"

When they finally made it to the woods they stopped to rest and plan the next move. Footfoot had a strange feeling come over him. He turned to look back towards the house, but it was nowhere in sight. "Hey ya'll look you can't see the house from here", said Footfoot. "Oh my goodness gasp Foot, "We've never been this far away from the house before I hope we can find our way back.

"Ah don't worry about that now we've got plenty of time to do think about that later.

"Lets go exploring", said Footfootfoot.

"Hey now don't run off now, Foot exclaimed, "We don't know our way around here and if you were to get lost we would never find you".

"Hey I know, lets go find "The Dark Lake" we've always heard about", said Footfoot.

"I don't know if that is a good idea we lost all out supplies", said Foot.

"Well we can look for the lake until we get hungry and then turn around", said Footfoot.

"Good idea Footfoot lets go", remarked Footfootfoot. So they set out for the lake. They had only been gone for a couple hours so they should have plenty of time thought Foot. The woods where nothing like they thought they would be. There was no danger like mother had said. It was beautiful, there were trees and flowers everywhere, birds were singing all around them, and squirrels were playing high up in the trees. It was great, so they quit worrying and headed for the lake. After a while they were still no closer to finding the lake. They looked for dragonflies, but there were none to be found. They listened for bullfrogs, but they heard nothing. They always saw dragonflies and heard bullfrogs when they went fishing with Mr. Groundhog thought Foot. He didn't worry Footfoot and Footfootfoot with it they were having so much fun he didn't want to spoil it for them.

"Hey do ya'll hear that", ask Footfootfoot?

"What", ask Foot?

"It sounds like someone crying", said Footfootfoot as he ran ahead to see what it was.

# Chapter four

# "A new friend"

Sure enough it was someone crying. There sat a little squirrel at the bottom of a tree crying it's eyes out.

Footfootfoot said, "hey little squirrel what's wrong"?

The little squirrel said, "I fell out of this tree and can't climb back up.

"Why not, did you hurt yourself when you fell", ask Footfootfoot as he looked up the big tree?

"No that's not it, said the little squirrel, if I tell you will laugh at me". Foot and Footfoot came walking up. "What is it", they ask?

"Well this little squirrel fell out of a tree, Foot tried to explain, but she won't tell what happened. She thinks I will laugh".

"Of course we won't laugh, we would like to help", replied Foot.

"Let us start by tell you our names. This is my brother Foot, I'm Footfoot, and that is my younger brother Footfootfoot", said Footfoot.

"Very nice to meet you my name is Puffy", said the little squirrel.

"Well now that we know each other why don't you tell us what happened so maybe we can help you and I promise we won't laugh", said Footfootfoot.

"Well I'm a little scared of heights. That is why I fell in the first place", mumbled Puffy.

Footfootfoot started to laugh.

"Oh no you better not we promised", said Foot as he went over and sat down beside Puffy.

"Yes with you being a squirrel and all I can see where that is going to be a problem", said Footfoot.

"What if we all stand around the bottom of the tree while you climb up. That might help you to feel safe", said Footfoot.

"Oh yes you could be right that might help. Here goes nothing", said Puffy. She looked down at Foot, Footfoot, and Footfootfoot as she climbed the tree and was at the top before she realized it.

"Yey! I made it and I wasn't even scared ya'll", yell Puffy down to the brothers on the ground. Puffy climbed back down the tree. "I'm glad ya'll came along and helped me. Ya'll are like big brothers, I feel safe now", said Puffy.

"Where is your mother", ask Footfoot?

"I don't know when I woke up this morning she was not there. That's what I was doing when I fell was looking for her", replied Puffy

"Well we can help you look for her on the way to the lake", said Foot.

"The lake, ask Puffy, is that where ya'll are headed"?

"Actually we were looking for it. We've never been there before", said Foot.

"I know where it is, said Puffy, come on and I'll show you". So they went Foot, Footfoot, Footfootfoot, and their new friend Puffy. They walked up hills, they walked down hills, they walked over logs, and they walked under logs. They walked until just couldn't walk anymore. "Should we have been there by now," ask Footfootfoot?

"I thought I knew the way, but everything looks different down here on the ground. I've always been up in the trees, I think I've got us lost", said Puffy.

"I thought you were scared of heights", replied Foot.

"Well not when I'm with my mother", said Puffy.

"I wish you mother was here now", said Foot. Puff started crying "I do too", she mumbled.

"I'm sorry Puffy I didn't mean to make you cry, let's forget about the lake and look for your mother," said Foot.

"She is probably worried about you anyway", said Footfoot. So they turn around and headed back the way they came.

# Chapter five

# "The search for Puffy's mother"

Thinking to themselves they all walked in silence a little way. Trying not to think about the fact they were lost and trying to focus on where to look for Puffy's mother. Foot said, "We need to go back to where we first meet Puffy and start looking there",

"That is a good idea we might find some clues", said Footfoot. So they hurried along headed to where they meet Puffy. "Wait a minute where I meet you is not where I lost my mother", said Puffy. "I had already been looking for her awhile before I got lost and fell out of that tree. So I sat down and cried and ya'll found me".

"Well I'm sure your mother has been looking for you by now and there is a good chance we will run into her on the way to where we meet you", said Footfoot.

"I really hope so", said Puffy, "I can't wait until she gets to meet my new friends too",

They started looking for thing they remembered seeing earlier when they first met. Puffy went up in the trees looking that big tree she fell from. Foot, Footfoot, and Footfootfoot spead out a little to look for track they may have left around the tree when they helped Puffy climb it. "This is it I remember the fork in it and the broke limb where I fell from", yelled Puffy! The brothers looked up to see which tree she was in and ran to it as Puffy was climbing down. "It sure is this is where we were all sitting", said Footfootfoot.

"Does anybody hear anything that sound like it might be my mother", ask Puffy?

"I'm afraid not", replied the brothers/

"We just came from that way, we came into the woods from that direction, and we've been down that trail", said Foot.

"In that case we need to spread out walking in that direction listening for anything sounding like it might be her mother", said Footfoot. So that is what they began to do. They could hear the bees bussing, they could hear the birds singing, and they could hear the wind blowing through the trees. But nothing sounded like Puffy's mother. They looked for what seemed like hours with no luck in finding her. So they decided to rest for a minute.

As they sat trying to catch their breath they heard something. "Quiet ya'll did you hear that", ask Foot?

"Yes it sounds like someone scratching a tree", replied Footfoot.

Puffy yelled, "mother, it's my mother" and she took off running toward the sound. "Hey wait for us", yelled the brothers as they went running too.

Much to their surprise when they found where the sound was coming from it was a tree with a hole at the bottom of it. Puffy yelled, "mother is that you in there"?

A voice said "I don't think so" and out popped a fox. "Well, well, well what do we have here", ask the fox? They were so scared they could not even speak. "The fox said, "don't be scared I won't harm you my name is Swindleton, Mr, Swindleton to you lads.

"My name is Foot, he is Footfoot, and that if Footfootfoot my two brother", said Foot.

"I see and who would this delicious I mean delightful little thing be here", ask the fox as he put his hand on Puffy's should?

"My name is Puffy and I'm looking for my mother. I couldn't find her when I woke up this morning", said Puffy.

"What a terrible thing to happen to such a sweet little thing like yourself, maybe I can help", said the fox.

"Have you seen my mother", cried Puffy. The fox thought for a minute. "Just a little while a go I saw her and it looked like she was hunting for something", replied the fox with a twinkle in his ete.

"OH please! Would you show me where it was you saw my mother Mr. Swindleton", begged Puffy?

"Well of course I will, that is what I do, I help lost little children like you lads. If you can just follow me I will take you to her", said the fox. Puffy was so happy to hear that, she ran over to Mr. Swindleton, grabbed his hand and said "lets go"! So off they went with the fox. This troubled Foot; he was getting a bad feeling about Mr. Swindleton. He didn't say anything he knew Puffy wouldn't listen. She wanted to see her mother so bad it wouldn't matter. The fox went on talking about how lucky we were to have ran into him and how he enjoyed helping us. After a minute Foot quit worrying about it and just followed along listening to Mr. Swindleton. He told them about helping some mice the other day hide from a hawk that was trying to catch them. "Really, a hawk, where di you hide them", ask Footfootfoot.

"We stood behind a tree and waited for him to fly by. Then we made a dash for my house just over the hill up there", told Mr. Swindleton.

"Then what happened", ask Puffy?

"Well after it was all over I had them stay for lunch", replied the fox.

"By the way you lads must be hungry, would you like to stop off by my house and grab a bite to eat", ask Mr. Swindleton?

"I don't know we need to get to Puffy's mother", replied Foot.

"Oh don't worry lad it's on the way and won't take but a minute. I already have the water on the stove", replied Mr. Swindleton. With a wink and a smile he turned and pointed ahead to a little wooden shack. "See their lads, not but a minute, then we'll be on our way to see your mother, little lassie", said Mr. Swindleton.

"I'm kind of hungry anyway and if it will only take a minute", replied Puffy.

"What about you lads", ask the fox?

"I guess so", answered the brothers. So they headed to Mr. Swindleton's for lunch. Right before getting to the front porch Foot started getting that bad feeling again, but this time he also felt scared.

"Stop ya'll something not right", whispered Foot. They all stopped dead in their tracks and looked at Foot.

"What is it, what do you think is not right", they ask? Foot motioned for them to come in closer. "I've got a bad feeling about going into his house", said Foot. The fox noticed they had stopped so he turned around and said "Hey hurry up now lads so we can have a bit of stew",

"We've changed our minds we just want to go no and find Puffy's mother", said Foot.

"What do you mean Foot we are hungry and I like Mr. Swindleton", whispered Footfootfoot.

"I don't care if you like him or not. We are not going in his house. I'm the oldest and I'm in charge", replied Foot. About that time Mr. Swindleton turned around and started toward them with a different look on his face. Not like the smile, his teeth were showing, this was a mean face. With a growling voice he said, "No I'm the oldest and I'm in charge". Before he could finish they heard another voice. One they have heard before.

"Hold it right there you good for nothing fox if you know what's good for you!" it was Mr. Groundhog.

"Well if it isn't my old friend the Groundhog, replied the fox, and what are you going to do?"

"Run boys I'll deal with this lying, stealing, rotten dog", yelled Mr. Groundhog. So they ran and hide behind a tree so they could still see what was happening. Then they heard something coming up behind them. Before they could see what it was they hear that voice. "Oh my boys are you alright", cried Mother Rabbit, grabbing them up and squeezing.

"Yes mother we are fine Mr. Groundhog saved us from Mr. Swindleton", replied the brothers.

"Mr. Swindleton is it. "That sorry fox was warned about messing with my boys", exclaimed Mother Rabbit in a very strong voice. She looks over where Mr. Groundhog and the fox were. The brother had never seen her this mad before. She hopped all over Mr. Swindleton. He couldn't get a word out. Everytime he would try to say something to Mother Rabbit she would hop on his head. Foot, Footfoot, and Footfootfoot could not believe their eyes. When she finally quit hopping on and kicking that sorry fox he ran like his pants were on fire. He didn't even stop at his house. He ran all the way out of sight. Thank goodness for Mother Rabbit and Mr. Groundhog thought the brothers and Puffy on the way to her with their arms wide open. "Oh Mother Rabbit are we glad ya'll came when you did", said the brothers.

"How did you know we were in trouble", ask Footfoot?

"Mothers just know things like that, but we will talk about that later. Right now we need to get you boys home", said Mother Rabbit.

"By the way mother this is Puffy, she lost her mother this morning and we have been helping her look for her", said Footfootfoot.

"Bless you little heart I'm so sorry about your mother. You need to come on home with us. There are things we need to talk about too", said Mother Rabbit as she put her arm around Puffy, gave her a big hug, and old her everything would be all right. They made their way through the woods and across the field. At last they made it home.

# Chapter six

# "A new family"

Mother Rabbit fixed a big dinner for them. She knew everyone would feel better after a good meal. After dinner Mother Rabbit planned on them all sitting down and talking about what had happened earlier that day. She especially wanted to talk to Puffy about her mother. Footfoot thought about it to himself. He didn't feel like it was good news for Puffy. He could tell by the way Mother Rabbit took a deep breath and sighed after she told Puffy she needed to talk to her about her mother.

Foot and Footfoot were more concerned about what she wanted to talk to them about. Foot said to Footfootfoot, "I don' know what she is going to be more upset with us about. Us lying to her or going against what she told us about the woods".

"Well she was right it is dangerous even if you can't always see the danger", said Footfoot. They finished their dinner, went and say in the living room, and waited for the worst.

After Mother Rabbit finished putting away the food and washing up the dishes she came into the living room and ask Puffy is she wanted to go outside to talk or just talk right there in the living room? Puffy wanted to stay inside so Mother Rabbit ask the brothers to go outside for a few minutes while they talked. Foot and Footfootfoot noticed it too, the way their mother was acting and talking so softly. The last time she acted this way, Father Rabbit was took by hunters. That was a very sad day. Much like this day will end for Puffy. The brothers went outside to sit and wait for Mother Rabbit to tell them to come back in. They waited quietly for what seemed like forever. Finally they heard their mother call them inside. She used that same soft sad voice they heard when she called them inside to be told about their father. When the brothers made it in Mother Rabbit told them to go into her bedroom and they would talk there. On the way they could hear Puffy in the living room crying her eyes out. There was no longer any doubt what mother was going to tell them happened to Puffy's mother. The brothers went on into her bedroom, sat on the bed, and waited for Mother Rabbit. She had went back to check on Puffy before coming to the bedroom. "Well boys I'm sure by now you have figured out why your new friend is so upset", said mother. The brothers just nodded their heads yes looking at their mother for some sign of what next. Then she started telling them what had happened earlier that morning in the woods.

She told them how Mr. Groundhog had came over about two hours after they left to go to his house and help him. He wanted to take them fishing, not knowing anything about what they had told Mother Rabbit. She told them about how she almost had a heart attack after Mr. Groundhog told her the terrible news about Mrs. Squirrel. "So that's when you knew to come and kick some fox fanny right mother", said Footfootfoot? That's when they got "the look". That look every mother gives and every kid has seen. The shut up and listen look.

"Now is not the time to discuss how much trouble you boys are in when all gets back to normal", said Mother Rabbit. She took a deep breath "what do you boys think about me adopting Puffy, she ask, from what Mr. Groundhog told me she has no family?"

"Yes she does mother, she has us as a family", replied the brothers.

"I knew that would be your answer I just wanted to make sure before I ask Puffy if she would be all right with it. You know I wished for on little girl and I got my wonderful three little feet brothers", said Mother Rabbit with a big smile.

They all laughed.

"Well she finally went to sleep, bless her heart. We will wait until she gets to feeling better before we talk to her about it", said mother to the boys as they started settling down for the night.

The next morning Footfootfoot was the first one up. He couldn't wait to ask Puffy about Mother Rabbit wanting to adopt her. "What are you doing up so early Footfootfoot", ask Foot?

"I can't wait to ask Puffy about the adoption", replied Footfootfoot. By this time their talking woke up Footfoot. He rose up to hear what they were scheming this early in the morning. "What is up with Footfootfoot", Footfoot ask Foot?

"Well he must be crazy. Mother will be the one to talk to her about that, besides I'm sure she is still to upset to talk about it", said Footfoot. Foot got on out of bed and went to make sure Footfootfoot didn't wake her up. Nothing to worry about thou Mother Rabbit had already caught him and put him to work helping her with breakfast. As Foot entered the kitchen mother told him not to say anything to Puffy about the adoption. The day was going to be spent helping Puffy feel better and to try to deal with losing her mother. "And Foot you're the oldest so it's your responsibility to get your brothers to help with this", said Mother Rabbit

"Don't worry mother I think I can handle it", replied Foot.

"Well your going to have to, Puffy will need a lot of my attention until she feels safe again", said mother.

After breakfast the brother and Puffy went outside to play while until Mother Rabbit got done with putting away the breakfast mess. She thought they might all help her in the garden today. Hoping it might help Puffy to not feel lonely, like she has family. So they did, they pulled weeds; they hoed around the tomato plants, and watered it all when they finished. Puffy was quit for most of the day. Later she started talking a little about how nice Mother Rabbit has been to her, about what a great family the brothers have, and how lucky she was to have meet them. The brothers didn't know what to say so they just listened. Glad she was talking and in higher spirits they were scared of saying the wrong thing. Then Puffy turned around to look at them. "I want to ask ya'll a question but I don't know how", said Puffy.

"What do you mean, you don't know how, you don't know the right words or what", ask Footfoot

"No not that, I guess I'm scared of what the answer might be", said Puffy.

"Well just go ahead and ask. We promise we won't scare you with the answer", said Foot.

"I was wondering, do you think your mother would adopt me so I can have a wonderful family too. With out my mother I have no family at all", said Puffy

"Oh my goodness Mother Rabbit is going to be so happy when she hears this. She has been waiting for you to feel better to talk to you about letting her adopt you", said Foot.

"I wanted to ask last night. I had a dream that she already had. It made me feel so much better in my dream it work me up and I've been thinking about it ever since. That's why I was so quiet today", said Puffy.

So they all ran to Mother Rabbit to tell her the good news. The brother noticed a change in expression on Puffy's face while we were telling Mother Rabbit. You could tell it helped the hurt for Puffy and it gave the brothers a sister. As they sat down for their first dinner as a new family Puffy said "if my mother can see me from where ever she is now, I know she is happy for me".

# The End

# Blurb

This is a story about three little rabbits, Foot, Footfoot, and Footfootfoot. Who were planning a long journey across "The big Field" to the woods in search of "The Dark Lake". Their mother had always told them never to go to the woods it was too dangerous for little rabbits. They just couldn't understand why Mother Rabbit could not see that they were not little rabbits anymore. Well they thought they were not anyway. And that is where the adventure begins.